DRACULA
BEYOND STOKER

Issue 2.5

DBS Press

Dracula Beyond Stoker
Issue 2.5

Tucker Christine
editor

Edward G. Pettit
consulting editor

Published by DBS Press
ISBN - 979-8-9867340-6-4 (Paperback)
ISBN - 979-8-9867340-7-1 (e-book)
August, 2023

www.dbspress.com
www.draculabeyondstoker.com

Letter From the Editor to the Reader

30 July

My Dear Loyal Reader,

Dracula Beyond Stoker began as an attempt to build a database of stories, novels, and plays that use Stoker's characters, locations, and themes to celebrate and continue the world he created. That database is ongoing(never-ending) at draculabeyondstoker.com — currently with listings for over 250 Novels, 200 Short Stories, and 30 Plays.

The fun we had in compiling this information led to an appetite to escort more stories into the world, hence *Dracula Beyond Stoker Magazine*. But the difficulty and expense we experienced in tracking down older works for our own collections gave us a desire to bring some back in to print to make it easier for you.

"Another Dracula?" by Ralph Milne Farley was first serialized in *Weird Tales* in September and October of 1930. As of this printing this the oldest nontheatrical work we've found that utilizes or acknowledges Stoker/Dracula.

It came at a time when Dracula was just reaching its enduring popularity. The Deane/Balderston play was touring after a successful run on Broadway and the Universal film starring Bela Lugosi was about to be unleashed on the world.

Interestingly, "Another Dracula?" is not actually a Dracula story, but rather a charming vampire tale in which the characters are aware of Stoker's novel and use it as a sort of guide. This device would go on to become a time-honored trope, but appears to have started here.

We hope you enjoy this story, and we hope to bring you more lost classics in the future. And, if you're aware of a story that came before this, please let us know.

Tucker

"A huge bat clung to the horse's neck, sucking its life-blood."

1. The Mysterious Coffin

I wonder who's dead?" inquired Dan Callahan, driver of Yankton's sole taxicab, pointing at a long wooden box with brass handles, which lay on a baggage-truck on the station platform.

"Search me!" replied the station agent, without interest. "Look at the tag, if you're that curious."

But Dan quite evidently wasn't that curious, for he slouched into a chair beside the one in which the agent sat, against the only cool wall of the freight house. It was late afternoon — or, rather, early evening — of an unusually hot June day. There never was very much doing in Yankton, Pennsylvania, and less than usual this particular afternoon.

The taxi-driver took a crumpled package from one of his blouse pockets, fished out a crushed cigarette, replaced the package, tapped the cigarette on his chair, put the cigarette in his mouth, took off his cap, ran his finger around in the sweatband, found a match there, replaced the cap, and lit up. The station agent was already smoking a pipe. The two sat and puffed in silence, watching the coffin; not that they expected it to do anything worth watching for, but merely that it happened to be directly in the line of their vision, and hence was as easy to focus on as anything else.

The shadow of the freight home gradually lengthened in front of them, and objects in the distance took on a reddish tinge. The definiteness of the shadow became blurred, the red tinge faded out, and blue twilight began to fall. A faint warm breeze crept down the tracks. Bats fluttered in and out under the canopy of the station platform, in pursuit of flies and midges.

A clatter and a roar and a swirl of cinders, as an east-bound train swept by; then silence again, the oppressive silence of a warm summer evening. Heat-lightning played over the hills in the distance.

Dan Callahan, the taxi-driver, untilted his chair, arose slowly, and stretched his arms.

"No passengers tonight," said he, "so I guess I'll be going home to Maggie and the kids."

"Say, will you look at that!" interrupted the railroad man. "One of them bats is trying to get into the coffin."

Dan looked, and made the sign of the cross. Clinging to the edge of the box, close to the lock, was a small brown bat, fluttering as though with suppressed excitement. As the two men stared, another bat joined the first.

"They give me the creeps," asserted the agent, as, rising from his chair and shuddering, he switched on the platform lights.

"Hasn't it turned a bit cold?" asked Dan, shuddering too.

The squeak of automobile brakes was heard, and then a third figure rounded the corner of the freight house. The newcomer was a young man still in his twenties; erect, well dressed, with straight pointed nose, firm jaw, and pleasing smile.

"Hello, Doc," Dan greeted him eagerly. "How's my little boy?"

"I've just come from your house," replied the doctor. "You'll be glad to know that the little fellow is much better. Responding to treatment beautifully. I believe that I may safely say that he is out of danger."

"Doctor Crane," said Callahan fervently, "you're a wizard and a brick. I thought sure I was going to lose little Dan. You've saved his life, and if there is anything that I can ever do for you this side of hell, just ask me. That's all, sir."

"It's nothing — nothing," replied Crane deprecatingly; "merely my professional duty. And a great pleasure, I assure you. Such a manly little fellow."

"Say, Doc," interrupted the station agent, "will you look at them birds trying to get into that there coffin?"

"Well, well, so they are," replied Dr. Crane, jovially. "I wonder what's attracting them."

"And here comes the great grand-daddy of them all," added the agent, as a grayish bat of fully two-foot wing-spread swooped down out of the gathering dusk, hooked its wings onto the edge of the box, and snapped viciously at the two little brown bats already there. They fled squeaking, but still fluttered around in the vicinity.

"Hm," remarked the doctor, professionally.

"Must be one of these there umpire bats I've heard tell about," suggested the station agent.

Dr. Crane strode over to the box, and brushed the huge creature aside with one hand. The bat snapped at him, and then shambled to one end of the top of the box, where it crouched menacingly. The doctor stooped and sniffed at the crack.

"Elm," he ruminated. "Peculiar smell, very, but not at all what I expected. No wonder it attracts these little creatures. As public health officer, I must get it to the undertaker's at once. Who does it belong to?"

"Dunno, Doc," replied the agent. "Look at the tag."

By the light of the platform-lamps, Crane read aloud, "'Mr. Peter Larousse, Yankton, Pa.' Who is he, I wonder? There's no one of that name lives here."

"I am he," said a quiet voice behind them.

None of them had heard anyone approach. They turned, and saw that a fourth man had silently joined them. He was tall, well over six feet in height. Dressed entirely in black, with a short black Inverness cape across his shoulders, fastened at the neck by a single clasp of gold with jet stones. In his right hand he held a black stiff hat, rather narrowed at the top of the crown.

He was old, of an indefinable age, yet erect, and exuding power and vigor. Clean-shaven, he was, except for a drooping white mustache. His face was aquiline, with high-bridged thin nose and peculiarly arched nostrils. He had a lofty domed forehead, crowned with white hair, profuse except around the temples, where it was scanty. His eyebrows were iron-gray and massive, almost meeting over the nose, and composed of profuse bushy hairs. The mouth, so far as it showed under the heavy mustache, was fixed and rather cruel-looking, with peculiarly sharp white teeth. These protruded over the lips, whose remarkable ruddiness showed astonishing vitality for a man of his evident years. His ears were pale, and at the tops extremely pointed; the chin was broad and strong, and the cheeks firm though thin. The general effect was one of extraordinary pallor.

His hands, at first glance, seemed white and fine, but closer scrutiny disclosed them to be rather coarse — broad, with squat fingers. In fact, most of the features of his anatomy, although appearing delicate and refined at first, nevertheless suffered by prolonged examination.

His general appearance, however, was courtly, aristocratic, and foreign in the extreme.

But the most noticeable single item about him was his eyes: small, gimlet boring and bloodshot without being in the least bleary. The three men who had preceded him on the station platform laid the redness of his eyes to the setting sun; but the sun had long since set, and the platform was now illumined by its electric lights.

"I am Peter Larousse," he repeated, ignoring the rudeness of their stares. "Did I hear someone mention my name?"

"Pardon us, sir," replied the doctor. "You startled us. I am Doctor Crane, the village health officer."

Crane advanced, extending his right hand, but the stranger did not grasp it. Instead, he swung his hat across his breast, and made a courtly bow.

"You will excuse me, I am sure," said he, "for not shaking hands, as I have an unexplainable aversion to personal contacts. Well, you called for Monsieur Larousse, and here I am. What do you wish of me?"

"Is that your coffin?" asked the doctor abruptly, becoming a bit nettled.

The stranger frowned, then smiled quizzically.

"Yes and no," he answered. "If you mean am I inside it, the answer is no. But if you mean is it consigned to me, the answer is yes. I am not dead — yet."

He bowed again.

"Well, it will have to get to the undertaker's at once," asserted Crane. "It's a menace to the health of the community."

"In what way, may I ask?' inquired Monsieur Larousse, serenely.

"It is already attracting vermin," replied the doctor.

The large gray bat was no longer to be seen, but the two little brown bats had returned and were clawing at the lid.

"Ah, the darlings!" exclaimed the stranger gloatingly.

Striding over to the coffin, he shifted his pointed hat to his left hand, and scratched first one of the little creatures, and then the other, on the head.

"See," he said turning, "they like me. They know a friend. I love all animals, and all animals love me. I have a way with them.

But now to get down to business. You wish this coffin removed, doctor? So do I. What is the next step?"

"This is Mr. Daniel Callahan, of the Commonwealth Garage," introduced the doctor. "He can get his motor-truck at once. The undertaker, being an undertaker, can be found at any hour. This other gentleman is Mr. Bill Jones, station agent, who can release the shipment. And I am the health officer, as I have already stated."

"Ah, what a fortuitous conjunction of personages!" murmured Monsieur Larousse. "The arrangements sound excellent."

While Dan departed for his truck, and the agent unlocked the freight house and turned on the lights inside, Dr. Crane asked, "And what are your plans for the body? — that is, I assume the coffin contains a body."

Ignoring the implied question, the stranger answered, "It is, of course, to be buried — in your local cemetery, to be explicit. What formalities are necessary?"

"You will have to have a cemetery lot."

"I have such a lot."

"And a permit from the village clerk."

"I should like to see him at once, then."

"He will be in his office tomorrow morning."

"He shall have to see me this evening." asserted the foreigner imperiously. "I suffer from a disease known as *dermatitis exfoliativa tropiea.* You, as a physician, will realize that that means I must avoid the daylight as much as possible. Can not the clerk, for a fee, be induced to transact official business in the evening?"

"I am sure he can," agreed the doctor smiling, "when I tell him about your disease. Would you mind my offering you my professional services? The exact sort of dermatitis which you mention is a rare disease, at least among white people; I have never had the privilege of treating, or even observing, a case."

"Then I refuse to be experimented upon," replied the stranger, drawing himself self up haughtily.

Just then Dan Callahan returned with his truck, and the four men put the box aboard. The box was unusually heavy, which rendered all the more noticeable the effortless ease with which the stranger handled his quarter of the load.

"Gosh!" exclaimed the agent, wiping his forehead. "It must weigh a ton."

"Ah, my friends," explained the stranger, "there is a lead lining inside."

"Then how the devil did the smell get out?" blurted Dan.

The stranger glared at him, and said nothing.

"Will you ride with me?" invited Dr. Crane.

"Thank you, no," replied Larousse with a slight inclination of his head. "The night is beautiful. I will walk — Oh, just a moment. One more question. Need the coffin be opened by any one?"

"Not if you have the death certificate with you."

"I have the certificate."

So the truck and the doctor's car drove away up the street toward the center of the village. The station agent re-entered his office to put out the lights. And a large gray bat hovered around the coffin in the departing express-truck.

The center of the village, a typical one-street Pennsylvania valley-town, was a bustle of early summer evening activity. Stores alight for the evening trade. Music issuing from the open doors of the movie-house. Couples strolling back and forth. Groups chatting at the street corners.

The gray bat did not follow the coffin into the bright lights of Yankton's gay white way.

Dr. Crane and Dan Callahan found the undertaker's wife at home, and she sent one of the children out to locate her husband. When he finally arrived, the three men tried to move the coffin, and were having a terrible time at the task when a calm voice near them said, "Permit me to assist."

It was the tall stranger again. With his help, they moved the box with surprising ease.

Next Dr. Crane and Monsieur Larousse hunted up the village clerk, got him down to his office, and secured the necessary burial permit.

When this formality was over, "Where are you staying?" the doctor asked.

The stranger drew himself up.

"That, my dear sir," said he frigidly, "concerns no one but myself."

The young doctor hastened to apologize.

"I only thought we might need to locate you, sir, if there should be any hitch in the proceedings," said he.

"There will be no 'hitch,' as you call it," replied Larousse, frigidly. "I have made all the necessary arrangements with the undertaker, and he assures me that there can be no unexpected complications. I shall remain in this beautiful little town for a considerable while. You will find me every evening somewhere along this street."

And bowing ceremoniously, he stalked off.

"After all that I've done for him," said Crane to himself, "he might have been a little more polite. A queer, queer man. My, what a spooky evening!"

The big gray bat swooped by, in spite of the bright lights, startling the doctor out of his revery.

2. Introducing Mr. Fulton

A bit later in the evening, the tall stranger entered Morton's General Store and made a few purchases. The news of the arrival of this mysterious foreigner had spread up and down the street, and now a crowd gathered to get a good look at him.

In paying for his purchases, be lingered quite a while at the cashier's desk. Who wouldn't linger for a chat with Mary Morton? She was by far the most radiant creature and wholly desirable bit of femininity that the little village of Yankton had ever produced.

A brief description of the town will not be amiss. Yankton, Pennsylvania, boasts one thousand odd inhabitants. They are quite odd, and Yankton does not boast them very loudly.

It is a typical old-time New England village. This may seem to be a strange statement to make about a Pennsylvania community, but New England itself is now overrun by practically every nationality of Europe. The people of old English stock there have lost their control of everything, except some of the financial centers of State Street, and the social centers of Back Bay. In *fact,* they have been forced to recognize the Irish, most of whom came over in the 1840's to build the railroads, as allies of theirs against the later comers, whom they regard as non-American.

But years ago, in Revolutionary times, the mountains of Pennsylvania and Ohio were settled by New Englanders of the original stock. Here you will find the purest *forms* of New England Colonial architecture. Here the Yankee blood has remained practically uncontaminated, right down to the present day.

But they had inbred and degenerated, for all of that. Individuals of marked mentality had moved away. The result was that the inhabitants of Yankton, although superficially prosperous, well-dressed and modern, were mentally and morally in the same dam with the superstitious illiterate mountaineers of other states and other parts of Pennsylvania itself. All that kept them from hex-murders and witchcraft-trials was a wholesome fear of ridicule; for they were just educated enough to know that such things are frowned upon in more cosmopolitan communities. In fact, it should be remembered that the New England forebears of these Yankton folk had had their own period of hysteria over witchcraft.

Mary Morton represented the flower of the pure old English stock. She had reverted to type, after generations of decline. She was the aspiration of all the young men of Yankton, and so she had been able to pick for herself the catch of the town, Herman Fulton.

Herman had had his eye on the main chance all his life. At an early age he had gone to work in the Yankton Bank, scorning a college career, or even the completion of high school. There were no college men in Yankton, except the two doctors. Not that Yankton men did not ever go to college, but merely that those who went to college never returned to Yankton; they went on to wider fields, where they made their long-slumbering heredity tell. Yankton could name with pride many of these distinguished sons of hers, men of national repute, who had turned their backs on their boyhood home.

But Herman Fulton had been different. He had stuck to the bank, had spent next to nothing, and had invested and reinvested his earnings to advantage. At the age of thirty-five, still a bachelor, he had worked up to the position of assistant cashier. Not that this indicated that Herman was possessed of any particular degree of intelligence. In fact, it is probable that he was subnormal mentally. Even morons are often fiendishly clever along some one line, and Herman possessed a well-developed money sense, if no other. True, he was self-educated and was an avid reader of books on all subjects, but it is to be doubted if he really understood very much of what he read, although he passed for quite a learned man in Yankton.

When the cashier had conveniently died, soon after Herman's attaining the position of assistant, Herman had demanded his place — and had been refused. At the next annual meeting he had calmly ousted the surprised board of directors, who did not realize that certain controlling blocks of stock, standing nominally in the names of old Dr. Porter and others, were really Herman's; had substituted a board of his own henchmen, and had elected himself not cashier but president!

After that, whenever Herman Fulton "requested" anything in Yankton, the request was usually granted, even if the granter couldn't quite figure out just what Herman intended to do if the request were refused. Herman was conscienceless and ruthless. Thus he speedily became the financial power of Yankton.

So all the girls, who for years had been setting their caps for him, had been intensely jealous when Mary Morton's parents had announced her engagement to Herman.

And then Dr. Ralph Crane, fresh from Harvard Medical College, had come to town, just about a year before this story begins. He had picked out Yankton as a likely place to build up a country practice, and had been welcomed by old Dr. Porter, who had more patients than he could handle at his advanced age.

Unfortunately, young Crane had fallen in love with the beautiful Mary, and it was evident that she liked him very much. In fact, if he had arrived on the scene before her engagement to Herman Fulton, there can be little doubt that the dashing young doctor would have speedily won her heart. But, in primitive communities such as Yankton, engagements are regarded as being almost as sacred, as marriages. In fact, they are usually lived up to a lot better. Engaged girls don't even dance with, or receive calls from, young men other than their fiancés. So Ralph Crane had had to content himself with worshipping from a distance, and with such professional contacts as occasional illnesses in Mary's family gave him. Mary herself was always the picture of health.

Entering the Morton Emporium on the evening in question, Dr. Crane observed with displeasure the quite evident regard which the courtly European was displaying for Mary, and the flattered interest which she returned. He would speak to Herman Fulton about it!

But, on second thought, he decided *not* to speak to Herman after all. If this old beau could make a dent in Herman's hold on Mary, so much the better. It was something that he, Crane, would have liked to do himself, if he had not been deterred both by respect for the local conventions and by fear of Herman's power.

At that, however, there was something about the performance which jarred on the young doctor's sensibilities, in spite of all his pleasurable anticipations of his rival's discomfiture. It may have been the May and December aspect of the situation. Or it may have been something else, some mere instinctive feeling. Perhaps the uncanny events, which had accompanied Monsieur Larousse's arrival, contributed to Dr. Crane's uneasiness.

Had Monsieur Larousse really "arrived"? This seems a strange question, in view of the fact that here he was. And yet, in the course of the evening, gossip developed the fact than he had not been seen to alight from any of the trains which had stopped at Yankton that day, nor had he got off the Lancaster bus, nor had he come in his own auto. Yet here he was, so he must have arrived — somehow.

The tall old gentleman lingered in the Morton store until closing time. Mostly he wandered up and down the aisles. Occasionally he would make small purchases. Whenever opportunity offered, he would chat with Mary. His attitude toward her was courtly and unexceptionable.

Morton's had many customers that evening, but Monsieur Larousse did not seem to notice that he was the center of attraction, the cause of unwonted crowds in the usually sparsely patronized store.

When Pop Morton finally put up the shutters, no one happened to notice where the stranger went. He did not register at the Republican House, nor did he put in an appearance all the next day.

Around noon, Dr. Crane ran across Dan Callahan on the street. Dan was in his cab, the doctor on foot.

"Hop in," shouted Dan, drawing up by the curb, "and I'll take you wherever you're going — free. I've something to tell you."

"Not that Junior is worse, I hope?" said the young doctor, as he got in.

"Heavens, no," replied the taxi-driver. "Junior couldn't get worse with you tending him, Doc. No, it's about the old bird whose coffin we moved yesterday."

"Not ill, is he?" asked Crane, professionally interested, and a bit hopefully.

"Not as I know of," replied Dan, "for he ain't been seen since the stores closed last night. No: it's about his coffin. They buried it this morning, without any service, and in the *Wilson* lot!"

"Well?"

"You know old 'Aunt Hattie', the witch who lives in that little cottage just beyond the cemetery? Lives all alone except for one big black tom-cat?"

"Well, she's a Wilson. And it's her who owns the Wilson lot."

"Hm," ruminated the young doctor. "Bats, and coffins, and black cats, and witches, and burial without church rites. It does sound a bit spooky, doesn't it?"

"It sure does, Doc!" agreed Dan, solemnly.

But neither of them could advance any theory as to where Larousse spent his nights.

3. Eavesdropping

That evening, as soon as the sun had set and the bats were out, out came the elderly stranger as well. For some time he walked the streets, furnishing the subject of conversation for whispering groups. Then, as before, he entered Morton's store, and resumed his attentions to Mary.

His attitude was courteous and respectful. Not a word, not an action, nor even a glance, that any one could take exception to. He evidently had traveled extensively, and he talked interestingly of all the countries of the world.

To Mary Morton, cooped up all her life in this little one-horse Pennsylvania mountain town, and — since her engagement to Herman Fulton — deprived of all other male attention, this elderly stranger was a diversion, in fact almost a god-send.

Herman usually spent his evenings in his office in the bank; but tonight, due to several anonymous phone-calls in several female voices, he abruptly left the bank, dragged his fiancée out from under the very nose of the elderly stranger, and huffily took her to the movies, thus depriving her father of his cashier for the rest of the evening.

Peter Larousse promptly faded from the scene. His chauffeur had arrived in town with an expensive foreign car, and this evening drove him out into the country. The chauffeur had registered at the Republican House, and the car was kept in the hotel garage. But Larousse himself did not put up at the Republican House. His own lodging-place still remained a secret.

The next morning, as Dr. Crane dropped into the Morton store to make some sort of a purchase — a collar, perhaps — he overheard heated words coming from Pop Morton's private office in the rear. The young doctor wasn't a gossip or an eavesdropper, and accordingly would have scorned to listen in, had he not overheard the mention of Mary Morton's name. His secret infatuation for the beautiful girl now proved too much for him, and so he at once developed an unexplainable interest in some kitchen cutlery, displayed on a counter along the opaque-glass partition which shielded the proprietor's sanctum.

"Am I, or am I not, engaged to your daughter?" came from the other side of the wall in the unmistakable tones of Herman Fulton.

"Of course you are — of course you are," replied Pop Morton soothingly.

"Well, then," continued the young banker, "haven't I a right to object to my fiancée compromising herself with that fish-eyed old French lizard?"

"But she ain't compromising herself," objected Pop. "That fish-eyed old French lizard, as you call him, has been perfectly polite and respectful to her. Besides, he buys lots of things at my store; and lots of people come in here every evening to take a look at him. He draws more crowds here than any advertising display I've put on in years. And if Mary draws *him,* what harm's done, at least as long as he behaves himself?"

"It's got to stop! I demand it!"

"But why? Why stop me making money? Is that a sensible way to treat your future pa-in-law?"

"The future wife of Herman Fulton has got to be discreet. If she can't be discreet, I'll break off the engagement."

"Now, Herman," remonstrated Morton, "I'd hate to think you cared as little for Mary as all that. You wouldn't do anything like that, I'm sure."

"Well, perhaps not," admitted the banker, rather sheepishly. Then taking a new tack, "But do I, or do I not, hold a mortgage on your store?"

"Sh! Sh! For heaven's sake, Herman, don't be so loud about it. I don't want that mortgage broadcast all over the county."

"Why not? It's on record with the prothonotary up at the county seat, isn't it?"

The storekeeper ignored this question, and countered with "See here, Herman, you leave this Mooseer Larousse alone for a few weeks, and I'll be making enough off of him to pay up your damned old mortgage."

"Now, Pop, is that a nice way to speak of your mortgage, when I was so kind as to help you out and lend you all that money when you had to have it or go under? And it isn't a question of paying off the mortgage 'in a few weeks'; it's a question of paying off that mortgage *right now!* It's already overdue, and I demand payment. My engagement to your daughter stands, but it's the mortgage against Monsieur Larousse. Mary must stop acting as your cashier until that spooky old devil stops hanging around your store."

"Why do you call him a spooky old devil?" asked Pop Morton artlessly, seeking to divert Fulton from his line of attack.

"Because he *is* one!" replied the latter, momentarily diverted. "He comes here with a coffin, and all kinds of strange bats and things. Nobody knows who he is, or how he got here, or where he came from. He never shows up, except at night. He keeps under cover in the daytime, and nobody knows where or why."

Dr. Crane, listening outside, chuckled softly to himself. "I know *why*, even if I don't know *where*. It's that confounded skin disease he told me about."

Meanwhile Herman Fulton was continuing, on the other side of the thin partition, "And he buried his coffin in the Wilson lot, which belongs to that old black-cat witch, Aunt Hattie. He *looks* spooky, too. He looks like — why, do you know what he looks like? It's only just occurred to me. I've been reading a book I got out of the public library, called *Dracula*, by a man named Bram Stoker. All about a he-vampire, who was dead and buried, and yet came out of his coffin every night, and sucked people's blood, until *they* died and became vampires, too. This Dracula could turn himself into a bat, or a wolf, or a shower of moonbeams, in order to get at his victims. I'll bet this old bird is Count Dracula himself, or at least another vampire of exactly the same sort. He looks just like the way Dracula was described in that story."

"Ha, ha, ha!" exclaimed Pop Morton, with forced levity. "Well, that's a good one. Ha, ha, ha! A he-vampire, eh? Why, I thought vampires were only *shes*. That's the way they always are in the movies. And they don't bite folks neither. Ha, ha, ha! A he-vampire! Well, that's a good one."

"Don't laugh, Pop. I'm serious about this. I really am. This is quite a different kind of vampire. It would make your blood run cold to read that story. That man, Larousse, is a positive menace to this community!"

"Now, Herman," remonstrated Morton in surprise. "You don't mean to tell me that *you* take any stock in such a cock-and-bull yarn as that?"

"Yes, I do, Pop. That story is supposed to be based on medieval European traditions. These blood-sucking vampires were well known in the old days. I've looked up about them in the encyclopedia, too. Seriously, I believe the man's a menace. He ought to be run out of town."

And then Pop Morton committed the tactical mistake of saying, "But what's to prevent my making a little money off him, first?" thereby bringing the conversation bark to the argument from which he had just succeeded in distracting Herman's attention.

He bit his lip, but it was too late to recall the words.

"*What's* to prevent?" snorted the banker. "*I'm* to prevent. You take Mary right out of your store and keep her out, or — "

"But it'll cost too much to hire another *girl* to do her work!" interposed Pop woefully. "Entirely apart from the money I lose by losing this he-vampire's trade, you want me to lay out extra money hiring a substitute for my own daughter, who don't cost me nothing."

"Do you talk of *money* at a time like this, with your own daughter's health, happiness, life, and even soul at stake? Pop, I'm ashamed of you! But I'll tell you what I'll do: I'll pay the wages of the substitute, and not put it on the mortgage either. Actually pay it out of my own pocket. And then we needn't tell Mary any of the reasons for what we're doing. No need to hurt her feelings by letting on to her what it's all about. We can tell her that I'm doing it as a special present to her, and because I object to the future Mrs. Fulton occupying a menial position, even in her own father's store. *My* wife must be free of all degrading toil."

"But think of all the trade I'll be losing," Morton objected feebly.

"Trade be damned!" snapped Herman.

"Think of you daughter — and your mortgage," he added.

The two men emerged, and Dr. Crane hurried away from the cutlery counter.

As he left, he heard Pop Morton whisper, "Do you suppose he heard us?"

"Don't care if he did," replied Herman Fulton, but not in a whisper. "He's only a sawbones."

That night there was a new young lady at the cashier's window of the Morton Emporium. But when Pop put up the shutters and went home at nine o'clock, he found Peter Larousse seated on the front piazza in earnest conversation with the beautiful Mary.

4. *Werewolves and Such*

So it became evident that simply relieving Mary Morton of her job as cashier of her father's store had not been enough to put a stop to the objectionable attentions of the weird old foreigner, who, Herman Fulton insisted from the depths of his reading, must be the original vampire Count Dracula, or at least his double.

Deprived of the opportunity of chatting with Mary at the cashier's wicket, Monsieur Larousse called on her at her home.

Her father felt that, of course, he ought to report the matter at once to her fiancé. But he kept putting this off, due partly to a general irresolution of character, partly to fear of facing Herman Fulton, and partly — it must be confessed — to a sort of satisfaction that he felt in the coming-to-naught of all the trouble that Herman had caused him.

As a result, it was several days before Herman discovered how the land lay. Mary could not be blamed, for no one had ever warned her against the old Frenchman. So for several evenings in succession, Peter Larousse called on her, and was welcomed. As she had been accustomed to spending her evenings at the store, time now hung heavy on her hands. Her fiancé was busy down at the bank, making money, and so she welcomed the visits of the distinguished foreigner.

Although his personality was rather chilling and revolting, yet he did bring to her the fresh outlook of the outside world. He talked entertainingly of the far countries which he had visited. All peoples and all times seemed familiar to him. And Mary rapidly began to realize what a limited, narrowing and cooped-up sort of a place Yankton was, after all!

But one night Herman called to take her to the movies, and found Peter Larousse already there.

Herman was chilled with horror at first. And then he boiled internally at the thought that all the good money he had spent in hiring Mary's substitute down at the store had been utterly wasted, for it had given "old Dracula" an opportunity to see her even more intimately at home. Herman would have liked to make a scene then and there. In fact, he nearly did. But his long banking career had schooled him with the realization that making oneself ridiculous has a bad effect on business. And business was always uppermost in Herman Fulton's considerations. So, although with difficulty, he steeled himself to be courteous to the older man, and politely begged him to excuse Mary for a prearranged date.

The stranger, with equal courtesy, submitted. But his eyes sized up the young banker appraisingly.

The deferred "scene" took place in the Morton parlor later that evening, on the return from the show. Herman stormed, and Mary wept and had to be comforted. But finally, because she really did care for her fiancé, in spite of his peculiarities and his domineering manner, she agreed that she would always be "out" thereafter, whenever Larousse called.

Larousse called regularly every night for a week, and at last gave it up. Like the drunken man who was thrown out of a party three times in succession, he knew when he wasn't wanted.

From then on, he walked the streets rather aimlessly after nightfall. Sometimes he would drop into a picture show, or would sit in the lobby of the Republican House, or even would make assorted purchases at the Morton Emporium. But by now he had become a familiar figure to the people of Yankton, and he no longer excited their attention. To no one, except Herman Fulton, old Dr. Porter, and young Dr. Crane, was he any longer of any moment. The interest of the two doctors was purely professional, although he would not let either of them treat his strange ailment. Herman kept his weird theories to himself, for fear of ridicule, but he read everything that he could find on the subject of vampires, even sending to Philadelphia for books, when he had exhausted the bibliography of the Yankton Carnegie Library.

And anyhow, so far as known, Larousse hadn't yet bitten any one in Yankton. But he was never seen to eat any regular food.

Even if the mystery of the mysterious stranger hadn't grown stale, there now were other matters to distract the attention of the citizens of Yankton. It was an unusually dry summer, and the drought afforded an absorbing topic of conversation.

In addition to the loss of crops and the threat against the town's water-supply, there began to be a large and unexplainable loss of chickens. Traps were set every evening, and were found sprung every morning, and still the toll of fowls continued. Several people reported having seen a lone wolf in the mountains back of the town.

Peter Larousse dropped gradually out of sight. He seldom appeared downtown in the evening any more, but no one took particular note of this defection, so intent had they all become on the lone wolf, and the depredation of the chickens, which two phenomena were now quite generally linked together in people's minds.

More people saw the wolf. Several poultry-raisers sat up in ambush and got shots at him, but he seemed to bear a charmed life, and to be immune to their bullets.

Eventually a huge German police-dog was found dead in the hills; and from that time on, the wolf was not seen again, and no more chickens were stolen; but no one could persuade the people of Yankton that these events had anything to do with each other. They knew perfectly well, these Pennsylvania mountaineers, that the wolf had merely transferred his predatory operations elsewhere. Couldn't they tell a wolf from a dog?

As for Herman Fulton, he had his own theories on the subject, but he kept them to himself.

About the time of the end of the wolf episode, Mary Morton was taken ill, and called in Dr. Crane. The young doctor didn't mind this at all, until the case began to get serious. Then he became frankly puzzled with the situation.

In spite of a good appetite and the consumption of plenty of food, Mary began to lose weight and grew pale and wan. Tonics were administered, but they seemed to be only temporarily stimulating. Finally blood-transfusions were resorted to, and these soon had to become more and more frequent. It was evident that Mary was losing blood steadily and rapidly, and yet there was no apparent cause for this loss.

Peter Larousse reappeared in his old haunts. His health seemed to have been greatly improved by the bracing air of the Pennsylvania mountains.

5. Dr. Crane's Adventure

Finally, the young doctor prescribed a change of scene for his patient.

He recommended that she be sent to the seashore, and that specialists be called in. But her fiancé, although most solicitous, had a narrow provincial clinging to his native town.

"There is no spot in the world more healthful than the Pennsylvania mountains," he insisted. "Now that the wolf-scare is all over, let's put her in my cabin in the hills back of the town. I'll have the place all tidied up, and will hire Mr. and Mrs. Foss to take care of it. Pay for the whole performance myself, too. Mrs. Foss used to be a trained nurse before she married Josh Foss, so we'll be killing two birds with one stone."

Dr. Crane reluctantly had to acquiesce. Herman Fulton was not only boss of the town; he was boss of Mary Morton, too.

Mary seemed to improve slightly under the change, and Ralph Crane soon found that the remote location of the camp gave him an opportunity to spend an undue amount of time with his patient, without attracting attention or exciting any gossip.

Then Mary began to fail again. She became paler and paler, and more and more bloodless.

Her fiancé, in accordance with his theories, made her a present of a beautiful chased gold crucifix, inlaid with (what he said were) diamonds, which he begged her to wear all the time in memory of him. He hung the cabin with bunches of garlic; but as Mary happened peculiarly to be rather partial to their acrid odor, she did not mind, especially as she thought that he knew of this strange liking of hers, and was doing it on that account.

He puttied up all the window-cracks with what appeared to be bread-crumbs, and did not mention the fact that he had procured this material at the Catholic church down the valley. Mary and he were good Methodists.

Dr. Crane ascribed this puttying to the old New England superstition as to the baneful effect of night air. He remonstrated roundly on general sanitary considerations, but finally gave in when the nights turned suddenly colder with approaching autumn, especially as the cabin leaked air like a sieve, anyhow.

Ralph Crane spent long hours nearly every evening with Mary, except on the occasions when Herman Fulton was there. As a result, Ralph and Mary became very good friends. For the most part they talked of their pasts, than which there is no better way of getting well acquainted. The girl recounted all the personal details of her rather uneventful Yankton girlhood. The young doctor told of his city childhood, his boyhood on a New Hampshire farm, and his struggles to put himself through Phillips Exeter Academy, Dartmouth College, and Harvard Medical School.

Herman Fulton didn't seem to mind this intimacy. In fact a sick, weak, bloodless and somewhat petulant Mary rather bored him, in spite of his regard and concern for her; and so he was glad to have some one else — provided no scandal was involved — take off his hands the task of keeping her amused.

One evening when the doctor and the girl were sitting alone together in front of the cabin, the full moon and a soft whispering mountain breeze were most suggestive of the appropriateness of ghost stories; so Crane embarked on an apt tale of his New Hampshire boyhood.

"The farm on which I worked," said he, "was about two miles from the lake from which we got our water supply. There was a hot-air pump down by the shore of the lake, which pumped the water up to a tank beside the barn. That sort of pump is a very simple affair: a little fire-box, holding only a shovelful or two of coal, and then a single air-cylinder and piston about a foot in diameter on top of that, and then on top of the cylinder a heavy three foot flywheel. This was the engine layout I don't remember how the pump itself was hitched up — all we had to bother with was the engine. If that went, then the pump went too. You don't see many of that kind of pump nowadays."

"I never heard of one," the girl said.

Dr. Crane continued, "It would run all night on one loading of coal; that is, unless it happened to stop. When it stopped, you could tell up at the farmhouse, because the 'thump, thump, thump' in the pipes wouldn't sound any more. Then whichever of the farmhands' turn it was, would have to light up a lantern, trudge two miles through the woods down to the lake, climb up on the big flywheel, hang on to one side of it to give it a spin, and thus start the pump pumping again. Well, this particular summer, we were troubled with mountain lions."

"Real lions?" interrupted Mary.

"Not the kind you see in circuses," explained Ralph. "The kind that we had up in New Hampshire looked about like a lioness, only somewhat smaller and slimmer. Both sexes look alike. The male hasn't any mane. Sometimes they call this creature a mountain lion, or a catamount, cougar, panther, painter, puma, or what have you? Well, anyhow, two of them came down out of the north woods up by Mount Chocorua, and started stealing chickens, much like this wolf they had around here last month. Only these beasts occasionally took sheep, and calves, too. A boy friend of mine, Tolly Piper, was driving the cows home from pasture one day, when one of these lions jumped out of the bushes, picked up a calf right under Tolly's nose, and jumped back into the bushes again with it."

"Horrible!" murmured the girl.

The young doctor warmed to his story, and went on. "One day one of them walked right into an afternoon tea of summer folks. It calmly surveyed the scene, while all the people sat frozen to stone. Then it slipped quietly back into the woods again. And at night you could hear them calling to each other from one range of hills to another. A most weird sound!"

"Did you ever see either of them?" asked the girl.

"Saw both of them," was the reply. "One night around midnight I was lying awake in my second-story room in the farmhouse, listening to the howls, when I noticed that the voices of the two lions came nearer and nearer together, until finally they met in the woods just between the farm and the lake. Then the sounds got louder and louder. We had some tame foxes in a wire-netting cage just back of the house, and I could hear our poor little pets whimpering with fright. Then there came an unusually fierce scream from one of the lions, followed by a crash against the wires of the cage. Then another scream and another crash, as the other beast sprang. This was repeated several times, but after a time the two animals gave it up, and came toward the house. I could see them distinctly in the moonlight, which was as bright as it is tonight. They would walk a few steps, and then sit on their haunches, throw back their heads, and howl. One time they stopped directly under my window — I could have hit them with a shoe."

"Why didn't you?"

"Because I preferred to sit and watch them. Didn't want to scare them away."

"But why didn't you shoot them?"

"The farmer for whom I worked didn't let any of the farmhands keep guns. So the two lions finally trotted off again into the woods."

"But that wasn't the adventure you were going to tell me about, was it?" asked Mary, a bit disappointedly.

"No," replied Crane. "The adventure happened the following night. Again I was lying awake listening to the cries of the pair, as they called to each other from range to range. And again the two animals met between the farm and the lake. But this time their cries then ceased. What silent devilment were they up to, I wondered. And then I heard the pump stop. It was my turn to go down to the lake and fix it."

"You poor dear," murmured Mary. "How old were you?"

"Only eleven. Naturally I was scared to death, but I had to go, for it was my turn. I begged each of the other farm-hands, one by one, to go with me, but they all refused; so I lit a lantern and set off alone through the woods. Not a sound from the mountain lions. If only they would howl, so that I could tell where they were, and what they were up to! But they kept abso-lutely silent. Somehow I reached the lake shore, got the pump going again, and started back up the road toward home. I was just beginning to recover from my stupor of abject terror, when upon rounding a curve of the path, I saw in front of me two green spots of phosphorescent light. Instantly I stopped dead in my tracks, absolutely petrified."

"I can well believe it," interjected the girl. "You poor little kid!"

Dr. Crane continued: "And then the beast came toward me. At least I judged that he was coming toward me, for the two phosphorescent eyes seemed to get wider and wider apart. In an attempt at frightening him, I swung my lantern widely — and the lantern went out. I was alone in the darkness with that thing up the road. Yet still the two spots of light glowed, even though there was now no lantern for them to reflect. Instinctively I felt that this was strange, but I was too scared to do any real thinking on the subject. Wider and wider apart got the two eyes. 'What a huge beast this most be!' I thought. From a distant ridge there came the blood-curdling scream of a lion. Fascinated, I waited for the beast in front of me to answer its mate. But the answer came from an entirely different quarter, far away. 'Can there be *three* of them?' I wondered. And then, with a flash of inspiration, I stepped fearlessly forward, right between the two eyes which were facing me. They were nothing but two glow-worms crawling on the dirt of the road."

"Well of all the yarns!" exclaimed Mary, a bit exasperated. "Here I have been getting up a lot of sympathy for you, and you weren't any more in danger of being eaten alive than I am right now."

"But I really was frightened, terribly so," protested the young doctor, a bit apologetically.

There was a pause, while the two sat and watched the moonlight on the gently swaying treetops of the mountainside.

Then Mary asked, "You have spoken of the terrifying scream of the mountain lions. What was it like? Can you describe it to me?"

"That's a pretty big order," laughed the young doctor, "for a lion's scream is different from anything else I have ever heard. It's just simply horrible — makes the hairs stand up on the back of your neck, and brings out goose-pimples all over your body. The nearest thing to it that I ever heard was a little child once, shrieking with pain in a hospital. It's — It's — "

As he paused, groping in his mind for a simile, the calm night air was split by one single ghostly shriek, coming from the woods just below them on the mountainside.

Mary's pale face turned even paler, as she sat suddenly erect in her chair and convulsively gripped the doctor's arm.

"What — what was that, Ralph?" she gasped.

"That," replied he, "was a mountain lion."

Tensely the two of them awaited a repetition of the sound. But it never came. That single fearsome howl was the only one.

Gradually they relaxed again. "What will you do?" asked the girl solicitously. "I can't bear to have you go home through the woods, now that this has happened. You might meet that — that awful thing. And I'm scared to be left here alone with only the Fosses. You must stay with me, Ralph. Spend the night. Please do. Mrs. Foss can fix you up a cot somehow."

So Dr. Crane spent the night in Mary Morton's little mountain cabin.

6. Beef and Other Things

Of course, when Herman Fulton learned that the attractive young doctor had spent the night in Mary Morton's cabin, he was furious. Even the fact of the presence of Mr. and Mrs. Foss in the cabin, as chaperones, did not in the least mitigate his anger.

His fiancée had been compromised! He himself had been made ridiculous! To a banker or businessman there is nothing worse than ridicule. Many a man would let his business go to smash rather than run the risk of ridicule to save it; and here was ridicule to no practical end. Why, it might even result in a run on the bank!

The only way to save his face was to take some drastic action at once. Accordingly he did. He asked Dr. Crane to withdraw from the case; and when the doctor refused to withdraw, Herman fired him. Herman was in a position to do this, as he was paying the bills. Old Dr. Porter was placed in charge, instead. The reason for the change, as given out to such persons as had any right to ask, was that Dr. Crane had unduly terrified his patient by getting her off in a lonely shack in the mountains and then telling her ghost stories. Indeed, Mary was so frightened by that single unexplained piercing scream of a mountain lion, that she insisted on being moved back to civilization the very next day. Altogether, everything fitted in to make Herman's explanation sound most plausible. And really Dr. Crane was open to considerable censure for telling Mary the lion story in her condition and location.

He accepted his removal gracefully, and conferred lengthily with his successor, who brought a new viewpoint to the situation.

Old Dr. Porter, after a rather cursory examination of Mary Morton and a study of the case-history, announced, "This acute anemia appears to me to be due to some cause which we haven't yet fathomed. You were probably taught at Harvard Medical that anemia is a *disease,* but the more modern theory seems to be that it is a mere *symptom,* the result of one of a large number of varying causes, many of which have been run to earth, but many more of which still remain unexplained."

The younger doctor agreed.

"I'll admit," said he, "that you older men are apt to be more progressive than our generation. We accept as gospel truth what we were taught at the school, whereas you have been out in practice long enough to realize how little is really known of the human body. Hence you are more open-minded to new ideas than we. Have you any theory as to the underlying cause of Miss Morton's symptoms?"

"Not yet," replied Dr. Porter judiciously, "but I believe that I have at least discerned the group in which her ailment falls. Her bloodlessness seems to me to be due to some organism, some creature that is sapping her strength. I shouldn't wonder — "

He paused with a bit of embarrassment, and then went on, "You know, years ago when I was a young man just out of college, I made a trip to the Argentine. One of the horses, on a ranch where I was visiting, was taken ill. It grew weak and emaciated. During the daytime it would eat ravenously and seem to pick up strength. But every morning it would be weak again. I was frankly puzzled, and was interested in the case from a medical viewpoint, although I had never felt any leanings toward veterinary practice. But my host merely shrugged his shoulders, and accepted the situation with Spanish fatalism. Also he did not seem to care to discuss the case. Whenever I broached the subject, he would avoid it with a bit of a shudder, and would make the sign of the cross. Most of the ranch-hands acted the same way about the matter. Finally one of the cowboys, not quite so superstitious as the others, led me to the horse one evening, and pointed out a huge bat — 'vampire-bats' they call them — clinging to the horses neck, sucking its life-blood."

"There has been such a bat around Yankton all summer," interrupted young Crane. "Can it be — ?"

"Let me go on with my story," persisted Dr. Porter. "The bat fled before I could get my hands on it. I at once inquired why they didn't keep the bat away, but the cowboy replied, 'It is not possible, *señor,* for once a vampire marks its victim, the victim is doomed.' But I myself am not a fatalist. I insisted on putting the poor horse at once into a carefully screened shed. Nevertheless the bat got in and out, and the horse continued to fail. We blocked every hole, but we could not cope with the fiendish ingenuity of that vampire. So, as a last resort, I persuaded my friend the cowboy — by means of *'mucho dinero'* — to sit up with the horse and guard it at night; to try and shoot the bat, if he got a chance."

"Did that work?"

"Yes, it did for a while. The cowboy didn't even see the bat again. The horse rapidly gained in strength, and I was just about to taunt the Argentines that the vampire was not as omnipotent as they seemed to think, when one morning I found the cowboy asleep, and the horse dead, drained nearly bloodless!"

"But, doctor," objected Crane, "if anything like that were happening to Mary, she would know it, and there would be marks on her throat."

"Are you sure that there aren't marks on her throat?" demanded the older man, pointedly.

"N-n-no!" admitted Crane. "Have you observed any?"

"I haven't looked," Dr. Porter replied. "This idea hadn't occurred to me when I first examined her. And now, frankly, I don't care to disturb her, in her present nervous condition. Nor, for the same reason, have I mentioned bats to her. But we shall keep a careful watch, from now on."

"Well, to be equally frank with you, sir," asserted young Crane, "I don't place much stock in your bat theory. But there have been a great many strange carryings-on in Yankton this summer, and nothing would surprise me very much. Certainly we don't yet know what is the underlying cause of Miss Morton's illness."

So Dr. Porter, following out his hunch, next interviewed Mary's father on the subject.

"You haven't seen any vampire-bats around the house, have you?" he asked abruptly.

Pop Morton's jaw dropped, for he suddenly remembered Herman's weird theories.

"Vamp — vampire what?" he gasped.

It was Dr. Porter's turn to become surprised, for Pop's confusion was clearly indicative of something.

"Why, what do you mean?" asked the doctor.

"Nothing. Nothing," asserted Pop, much embarrassed. "No, I haven't seen any bats at all."

And nothing more could Dr. Porter pump out of him, except the repeated assertion that he hadn't seen any bats. Nor did Pop mention the conversation to Herman Fulton until much later.

Mary continued to waste away, recovering a bit sometimes for a week or so at a stretch, only to fall still lower the next time that a relapse set in.

Meanwhile Dr. Crane's patients steadily deserted him, one by one. It soon became evident to the young doctor that Herman Fulton, not content with removing him from the Morton case, was insidiously and persistently bringing to bear the bank's influence to drive him out of town, until at last the day came when the young doctor was unable to meet a payment on the mortgage on his own establishment, and was refused an extension by the banker.

Fulton then placed his cards on the table by offering a handsome settlement for the equity, if Dr. Crane would move out of town; and so Dr. Crane moved.

For some time past, one of the New York hospitals had been angling for Dr. Crane's services, and now he accepted the offer.

Herman magnanimously permitted him to say good-bye to Mary. The farewell was touching, though brief. Not a word was said to let the girl know that Crane was the victim of her fiancé's jealousy.

"I've a splendid opening in New York," reported the young doctor, "and so I am reluctantly leaving Yankton to take it. But the real impelling reason is that New York will give me an opportunity to read up on anemia, and I hope to find out some way of curing you. If I succeed, I shall be very glad that I left. In any event, please remember that I shall always be your devoted friend. Please, please call on me, if you ever need help."

Seizing her hand, he held it tightly for a moment, and then left abruptly. There were tears in the eyes of both of them.

I mmediately on his arrival at his new job Dr. Crane hunted up the member of the hospital staff who was supposed to know the most about anemia; and through his suggestions, plunged into a line of evening reading in the medical alcove of the New York Public Library.

He wrote Mary Morton once — merely a brief note, giving her his address, and expressing a hope that she was better.

It was not long before a solution of Mary's case began to dawn on him. He found that, as old Dr. Porter had stated, the modern trend of opinion is that anemia is always secondary. He found, to his surprise, that even more of the primary causes of that disease had been worked out and pinned down than Dr. Porter had intimated.

The enthusiastic young researcher compared each of the known features of the girl's case-history with the ear-marks of each of these various primary causes, one by one, until at last he hit upon what seemed to him to be unquestionably the uniquely correct solution.

Dr. Porter had been very nearly right in his surmise. There was now a chance to save Mary. So Ralph Crane rushed off the following letter by special delivery:

Dr. Jeremiah Porter,
Yankton, Pa.

My dear old friend,
I believe that I have at last hit upon the lying cause of Miss Morton's condition. Her symptoms, her case history, and the situation at Yankton seem to fit the specifications exactly. You were quite right in your hunch that she is the victim of a parasitic organism, but I do not believe that it is a vampire-bat.

The books describe a form of anemia, very similar to hers, and often found in mining communities. It is due to a parasitic worm, the *ankylostomum duodenale*, which inhabits damp places, especially underground mines.

The symptoms are very similar to those of pernicious anemia, for which we have been treating her; that is to say, successive remissions and relapses, with the nervous symptoms very marked.

May I suggest *santonin* for a time, in place of *blaud*
Let me know how the dear girl is.

Respectfully,

Ralph Crane, M.D.

Then anxiously he awaited an answer. It came bade two days later by wire:

Diagnosis too late. Mary died Monday. Funeral three o'clock tomorrow.

J. Porter.

7. Haunted

It was already tomorrow when the telegram arrived, announcing Mary Morton's death. Crane, stunned and heartbroken by the news, hailed a taxicab and rushed to the Pennsylvania station, only to find that there was no train which could possibly get him to Yankton in time for the funeral. So he sent some flowers by telegraph, and gave himself up to an afternoon of bitter recrimination.

He had failed the girl he loved. Oh, if he had but worked faster and to more purpose, and had found out the cause of her amble before that knowledge was too late to save her! Of course, his diagnosis might not be correct; and even if correct, it might not have enabled him to cure her. But there had been a chance, and that chance was now lost forever.

Later a letter arrived from Dr. Porter, but it didn't throw much more light on the situation. Marks and blood had been found on Mary's throat, but the girl had insisted that they had been due to her scratching a particularly vexatious wood-tick bite, which she had acquired in the mountain cabin. A constant guard had been set over her, but no bat or other animal had approached her, except a stray black cat which had jumped over her bed on the day of her death. The huge gray bat had been seen around town occasionally, but not near the Morton house. It all sounded rather banal and silly, when set down in black and white on paper; but, in view of the previous conference between the two doctors, Dr. Porter said that he felt duty-bound to state all these details. He expressed no opinion about the *ankylostomum duodenale*, except to thank Dr. Crane for the suggestion, and to express an appreciation for the younger man's zeal, persistency and thoroughness at research. All of which was most unsatisfying.

Young Crane was crushed, stunned and broken-hearted. His Mary was dead! His Mary was dead!

At last he realized that what he had mistaken for merely warm affection for the girl, had really been love. Oh, if he had but realized this in time!

It was his fault! Her death was all his fault! He ought to have asserted himself, have declared his love, and have dragged her away from Yankton to New York, where she could have had adequate medical attention.

For about a week, he drove his numbed brain and weary body. During working hours, his hospital duties afforded him some measure of forgetfulness of his grief; but at night there was no relief. He walked many miles every evening. Then he would lie awake in bed, the prey of bitter recrimination, until at last sleep came, but not oblivion, for even his sleep was tortured by dreams of what might have been.

And then one night, about midnight, he suddenly awakened with a feeling that there was someone in his room. He was thoroughly frightened, even before he started to awake; and yet be could not remember any dream which could be responsible for this feeling. Merely he waked up already scared, and with no apparent cause.

The room was quite light from the reflection of an advertising sign near by, and so he could distinctly see everything in the room. By the foot of the bed there stood a young girl clad in white, smiling down on him.

It was Mary — or Mary's ghost! But it couldn't be her ghost, for there are no such things as ghosts. So it must be Mary herself. But Mary was dead. But she couldn't be dead, for here she was. What was she doing in New York City? And in his room! And at this time of night! His Mary, at last! Could it be true?

"Mary!" he gasped.

"Yes, Ralph," the figure replied, "it is Mary. I have come to you for help, because Herman doesn't seem to understand. Night after night I have tried to get Herman to help me; but he only cringes, and makes the sign of the cross, and says horrid things to me, which I don't understand. He calls me 'undead'. Of course I'm undead! I'm alive, as alive as you are; but somehow he says the word 'undead' as though it meant something else, something terrible and unclean. I can't understand him, and he refuses to understand me. But you will help me, won't you? You promised me, you know."

"Of course I'll help you, Mary dear!" he exclaimed. "But what are you doing in New York? Just step into my sitting-room for a moment, until I get some clothes on."

She smiled wanly.

"I'm not in New York, Ralph," she replied. "I'm buried six feet deep in a cold dark grave in the Yankton cemetery. But I'm not dead. I'm sure of that. Sometimes I lie for hours in that awful padded coffin. Sometimes I sleep. Sometimes I lose my head, and shriek and struggle in the darkness, trying to tear the box away and get out. And sometimes I think very calmly and steadily of some place, usually Herman's room, until suddenly I find myself there. Then I plead with him to help me; but he repulses me, and drives me back into the grave again. I feel that I can't stand it much longer. Either my strength or my wits will give out, and then I shall be really dead."

It was quite clear to Dr. Crane that the poor girl was out of her mind. She had probably been in a cataleptic trance, had escaped from the coffin on the very eve of burial, and had closed and locked the box, perhaps even filling it with books so that her absence would not be noticed. Insane people are quite often diabolically clever in such ways. He remembered, from his recent extensive reading, that anemia often results in either catalepsy or insanity, so why not both? It was the only plausible solution!

His heart went out to her in a wave of masculine protectiveness. Here was a chance for him to give to the girl he loved the expert hospital care which she had lacked in Yankton, and to restore to her both her health and her sanity. Then let Herman try and get her away from him!

As the young doctor groped in his mind for soothing words to quiet her hysteria, she spoke again, "You will help me, won't you, Ralph? I frighten poor dear Herman so! He is beginning to get pale and anemic just like I was. Last night he had another man sleeping with him, and so I can't go there any more. It embarrasses me."

"Of course I'll help you," reassured. Dr. Crane. "Now if you'll just sit down for a moment in the next room, I'll be right with you."

"Thank you, Ralph," said she. "Good-bye. Come quickly! Very quickly!"

He rubbed his eyes. She was no longer there! And yet he had not seen her leave the room.

Dr. Crane got up and dressed, and walked the streets of New York until morning. He did not dare to go to sleep again, and thus establish the possibility that he had merely dreamed what had just happened to him.

He was standing eagerly on the steps of the Public Library when it opened at nine o'clock. As the doors were unlocked, he rushed to the medical stacks, where he plunged into a new line of reading, namely, "cataleptic trances."

By noon a smile of grim determination had settled over his features, and he had wired to Dan Callahan, the Yankton taxi-driver, to meet him at the Limited.

"A black cat walked across Mary's body."

8. In The Grave

Well, sir, you've come," exclaimed Dan Callahan, as Dr. Crane swung off the Limited late that night. "I got your wire, and here I am, although pretty near every other man in town is up at the cemetery. But not any of the women; for it's no fit work for a woman."

"What isn't?" asked the young doctor, with ominous foreboding.

"The gang is digging up Mary Morton's body."

"To save her life?" asked Crane, eagerly.

"Save her life? Naw!" replied Dan. "She's dead. But she's been haunting people all over town since she died, and so some of the men have got it figured out that she's turned vampire."

"She's turned what?" exclaimed Crane, astonished.

"Vampire," explained the taxi-driver. "Not the movie kind, but the spook kind, that flies around at night and sucks blood. Herman Fulton has been reading up a lot about them in the Carnegie Library, and it seems like there really is such a thing.

They reckon that that old Frenchman, Mussoo Larousse, is one too, and that his coming here had something to do with poor Mary dying and turning into one. He's been laying low ever since Mary died. But the gang is out to get them both. It says in the book, which Herman was reading, that the only way to cure a vampire is to cut off its head and stuff its mouth full of onions."

"Just a minute," interrupted the young doctor, horrified; "you don't mean to say that's what they're planning to do to Mary!"

"Why not?" replied Dan. "She's dead, ain't she? And besides, she really has been haunting people."

"Dan," said Crane solemnly, seizing him by the shoulders, and staring into his eyes, "I don't believe that Mary is dead at all. I believe that she's merely in a cataleptic trance — "

"Speaking of cats," interrupted the Irishman, "that's another thing. A black cat walked across Mary's body just before she died, and hasn't been seen since; and they say that that's a sure sign that both she and the cat have turned into vampires."

"What a beastly lot of rot!" exclaimed Dr. Crane, indignantly. "It's nothing but absurd superstition! There's a very good chance that Mary is still alive, and that all this so-called 'haunting' is merely due to her efforts to communicate with her friends and loved ones, and get them to rescue her. Whereupon they go and dig her up, not to save her life, but rather to kill her. My God, while we're wasting time talking here, they may be doing it already! Come on. Are you game to help me stop them?"

"That I am!" Replied Dan fervently. "You saved little Danny's life, and I'm with you in anything this side of hell.

"Have you any guns?"

"One automatic pistol in my cab, and another at the garage."

"Let's get them, then, and let's hurry. I have a revolver in my grip here."

Soon the two allies, fully armed, were speeding over the mile of road which led from the village to the cemetery. They found the burial-place crowded with men. Cars were parked all around.

Leaving the taxicab as near to the graveyard as they could get, they hurried forward with flashlights in hand, and weapons as yet concealed

"Thank God!" breathed Dr. Crane, for the digging was still in progress.

No one paid them any attention as they joined the milling throng. Many of the men carried lanterns, which they held high around Mary Morton's grave, while others took short turns with a spade. Little brown bats fluttered about in pursuit of the insects which the lanterns attracted.

It was evident that the digging had only just started. And every one was so excited that the hole did not make very rapid progress.

Dan Callahan had exaggerated. There were but few of Yankton's leading citizens present. Most of the mob consisted of coal-miners and others of the lower strata of the community. But there were enough of the higher strata present to make the gathering quite representative. In fact, a survey of the crowd would give a pretty good idea as to just what promissory notes, held by Herman Fulton's bank, were badly overdue.

Herman himself was in charge of operations. He fretted and fumed and scolded and interfered, none of which helped particularly to speed up the work.

Dr. Crane remarked in an undertone to the trod-driver, "We might just as well let *them* do the digging for us. Then we can step in at the last moment, and do the rescuing ourselves."

So the two lay low, remained inconspicuously on the outskirts of the crowd, and waited.

Finally, well toward morning, the crunching of the shovel changed to a wooden thumping. Every one heaved a sigh of relief. Their flagging interest revived. Presently the man in the hole passed up the lid of the box which contained the coffin.

"Now to open the coffin," said he.

"No you don't!" some one shouted. "Haul it up, and give us all a look."

"Yes, yes," chorused the crowd. "Haul it up. Give us a look."

So ropes were attached to the handles, and the coffin was hoisted onto the ground beside the grave.

Herman Fulton bustled authoritatively forward.

"Undertaker here?" he inquired.

"Yes, sir," a voice replied.

"Got your keys handy?"

"Yes, sir, but we haven't any permit from the Board of Health."

"You should have thought of that earlier in the evening. The clerk will back-date a permit tomorrow, if I ask him to. A public duty, like what we are doing tonight, can't wait on any formalities."

"Yes, sir."

And the undertaker stepped forward and unlocked the coffin. Herman started to raise the lid, and then hesitated. Dr. Crane and Dan Callahan gripped their pistols tighter, and surged forward with the crowd that pressed expectantly in from all sides.

Herman said, "Now don't be surprised if the coffin is empty, for she may be off right now on one of her vampiring trips. If so, we'll just have to wait until she returns, which she's sure to do before morning. I've been reading up a lot on the subject, and I've found out that vampires must always come back so their coffins before sunrise."

So saying, he flung up the lid. But the coffin was not vacant. There lay the body of Mary Morton, just as when the coffin had been dosed several weeks before. No ravages of decay were in evidence. A delicate pink bloom lay on her cheeks. Her lips were red. She looked almost like her old-time self of before her illness.

The crowd gasped in unison. Then some one exclaimed, "She looks alive!"

"Why wouldn't she?" muttered the undertaker under his breath. "I rouged her up good for the funeral."

"Is she really dead?" asked some one.

"No," replied Herman Fulton authoritatively. "Haven't I explained it to all of you again and again? She is what the books call 'undead.' She is a vampire. This Larousse person is one, too. Vampires go on living after they die. They sneak out of their graves at night to haunt people and to suck people's blood. And when their victims finally die, the victims become vampires in turn. Larousse sucked Mary's blood until she died and joined his band of devils. She is now haunting several of us, though she doesn't seem to have bitten any of us yet. If we don't free her, we'll become vampires when we die, and so on. It's a vicious circle. It's — it's like one of those chain-letters: once it gets well started, there's no telling where it will end up. We've got to stop it right now — nip it in the bud, as it were."

He spoke his piece like some patent-medicine faker getting off a line of patter.

But Pop Morton blurted out, "I dunno, Herman. I've heard all your arguments again and again. But it's contrary to nature for me to let you mutilate my daughter's body. Sacrilegious, too, after she's been given a Christian burial."

"Mr. Morton," said Herman sternly, "your daughter herself will be grateful. Her poor spirit doesn't enjoy being a vampire. It longs for rest. We must cut off her head, drive a stake through her heart, and fill her mouth with garlic. Then you will see a look of peace descend upon her sad face, as her spirit is released from its thralldom, and returns to God who gave it."

"Her face do look sad," interjected someone.

"No wonder," muttered Dr. Crane under his breath.

Herman Fulton continued sententiously, "I was her fiancé, and so it is my right and duty to strike the blow that sets her free. I hate to mutilate the beautiful body of her whom I loved. But I know that it would be her own wish to have it so. In a few moments she shall be freed from the devil. And then we shall dig up that devil himself, over in the Wilson lot, and free him, too, though not for any love, in his case, but rather merely that his evil career may be put to an end. Mr. Morton, in a few moments, loving hands will send your daughter's soul to peace."

Herman Fulton drew a long hunting-knife from his belt.

"Stop!" shouted a voice in the crowd.

Every one looked around, some holding their lanterns aloft and shading them to see who had caused the disturbance. They looked into the drawn revolvers of Ralph Crane and Dan Callahan.

"Stand back there from that coffin! Quick! All of you!" commanded the young doctor, dipping his words off peremptorily.

The crowd recoiled immediately and instinctively.

But Herman sneered, "So it's little sawbones come back for his sweetie! Do you want to claim for yourself the right to save her soul?"

"I claim the right to save her *life,*" replied Crane tersely.

"Any, more wise-cracks out of you, Herman Fulton," added Dan, "and they'll be your last remarks this side of hell."

Herman glowered, started to say something, then thought better of it, and remained silent.

Dr. Crane continued, "You've all been listening to the most arrant lot of bosh and medieval superstition. Mary Morton isn't dead, she's merely in a cataleptic trance. If you idiots will keep out of the way for a few moments, I can resuscitate her, and prove it to you."

"No you don't," asserted Herman Fulton. "We've got to act quick. The first thing you know, she'll vanish in a shower of sparks, or a black mist, or turn into a bat or something, and make her escape We're wasting time talking."

"Yeah?" remarked some one from the crowd. "Well, you said yourself that she'd have to come back at sunrise. So what's the difference? Let's give the Doc a chance."

"Yes, let's," echoed several others.

Herman was nonplussed for a moment. But then, remembering that he was the banker who held most of their financial lives in the hollow of his hand, he recovered his poise. He stared imperiously round at his followers. One by one, as his glance fell upon them, they remembered some mortgage, or note, or over-drawn account, and their incipient opposition crumbled.

The crowd was angry and chagrined at Herman's power over them, but they dared not vent their anger upon him, and so they looked around for a vicarious victim, and finally centered on Dr. Crane. The mob began to murmur.

The doctor sensed their growing unrest, and realized that they were rapidly working themselves into a fanatical condition, in which they would attack him and Dan, in spite of the auto-matics. This would mean shooting to kill. Dr. Crane had no de-sire to kill any one, and besides he wanted to be sure and save Mary Morton. Oh, if there were at least two men in the crowd whom he could trust to hold his revolver and one of Dan's while he himself tried to bring Mary back to life!

"What's the disturbance?" asked a quiet voice behind him.

The answer was an angry snarl from the mob, as Monsieur Larousse, in his inevitable cape-coat, stepped to the side of Dan and the doctor.

"It's the old devil himself," snarled Herman Fulton.

"That remark appears to be addressed to me," said Larousse with imperturbable suavity. "Will someone please explain."

"You don't need any explanation, you old vampire," blurted out Herman. "You know yourself that you are one of the undead. You sucked the blood of Mary Morton, and made a vampire out of her, too. So we've dug up her body, and are going to drive a stake through her heart, to lay her ghost The night is nearly over, and then when you return to your own coffin with the morning light, we'll drive a stake through you, too."

"I take it, sir," said Larousse, ignoring Herman and addressing Dr. Crane, "that you are not in the least impressed by this tommyrot and poppycock. You and the taxi-man here appear to be opposing these gentlemen. You look sensible. Is there anything that I can do to assist in preventing this sacrilege? Little Mary Morton was a dear sweet girl, whom I greatly admired."

"We know you did," sneered Herman Fulton.

Dr. Crane felt a bit uneasy at having this suspected Dracula-person for an ally. But it was a case of any port in a storm.

"We have three guns," said he. "If I can get two sane individuals to help me, Dan and they can hold back the mob, while I have an opportunity to bring Mary out of her trance."

"Doctor," said Pop Morton, stepping forward, "I'll take one of the guns. You're a doctor, and you ought to know what you're about."

With a sigh of relief, Crane handed over his pistol. But instantly a crafty smile played across the features of Pop Morton.

"Stick 'em up!" he shouted. "Crane, Larousse, Callahan! Let go your gun, Callahan!"

He had the drop on them all, even on Dan, who promptly let go the one gun which he held. His other automatic was in his pocket.

"Now do your dirty work, Herman," exclaimed Pop, rather pleased to be usurping Fulton's center of the stage. "Quick, while I hold off these interferers."

9. The Tables Turned

But even as Pop Morton spoke, a gray arm was suddenly swung around his neck from behind, while at the same instant the other hand of his assailant seized his right wrist and elevated the muzzle of the gun. Dr. Crane leaped forward and swathed away the weapon.

Meanwhile, however, Herman Fulton, taking advantage of the diversion, had sneaked up to the coffin, with drawn hunting-knife, which he now held poised aloft over Mary's breast.

"No you don't!" sang out Dan Callahan, whipping out his other gun. "Back from that coffin, you dirty rat."

Herman quickly obeyed.

Monsieur Larousse addressed the man who was holding Pop Morton. "Ah, Higgins, you arrived just in time."

The newcomer was his gray-uniformed chauffeur.

"Now, doctor," announced Larousse, with a grin which revealed his white fangs, "you have the two sane men for whom you wished, namely, myself and Higgins. And I have a little pistol of my own, so you are still one gun ahead. I suggest that you proceed with the resuscitation at once, before some one else tries to stop you. That old fool of a storekeeper nearly succeeded, you know."

So saying, Larousse pulled out a pearl-handled thirty-two, and his chauffeur picked up the gat which Dan Callahan had dropped. Four well-armed and resolute men now surrounded the coffin and held the crowd at bay.

Herman Fulton felt his prestige rapidly evaporating. Something must be done to retrieve the situation!

"Just a minute," he remonstrated, holding up his hand. "Let's talk this thing out, like reasoning human beings. You don't look at all at ease in your own mind, Dr. Crane, at having Dracula for an ally, so — "

"Dracula?" cut in Larousse. "So *that's* what you've been reading! Bram Stoker, who wrote that infernal book as a mere bit of fiction, has a great deal of innocent blood on his head. I wonder how many superstitious mobs in back-woods communities have dug up the bodies of cataleptic sufferers and spiked their innocent lives away, since that damnable novel was written, instead of digging them up and resuscitating them!

"I speak with feeling," he added. "For some of the men in my club in Paris used to taunt me with the nick-name 'Dracula', because of my supposed resemblance to the hero — or rather, villain — of that story."

"But you *are a* vampire, aren't you?" objected Herman.

"Certainly not!" replied the old man, a bit testily at last.

"Then who is buried in that coffin over in the Wilson lot, if it isn't yourself?"

"My father," said Larousse with a touch of reverence in his voice.

"And who was your father?"

"Tom Wilson. Did any one here know him?"

There was a murmur of surprised assent from some of the older men, one of whom added the information, "When Tommy was just a boy, he was run out of town for robbing the till at the feed store."

"It's a lie!" shouted Larousse, his red eyes blazing in the lantern light. "My father never robbed that till! He was falsely accused, and had to flee or go to jail. So he ran away to sea, and changed his name to Larousse — took the name of his ship captain. Finally he ended up in Paris, established a trading firm there, became very rich, and married. I was his only son. He had me educated at British and American universities. When he died — my mother having predeceased him — he left me his fortune, contingent on my burying him in his old home town, which he seemed to love in spite of the unfair way in which it had treated him — I don't know why I am telling you all this, for it certainly is none of your concern."

Herman Fulton exclaimed under his breath, "It's the gift of the gods! If we can keep that old bird talking until sunrise, we'll have him at our mercy." So he asked aloud, "But you don't live anywhere, and you come out only at night. Where do you sleep in the daytime, if not in that coffin?"

"As to my coming out only at night, it is because I suffer from tropical dermatitis — v"

"I can vouch for that," interjected Dr. Crane. "Tropical dermatitis is curable only if the sufferer keeps away from the ultra-violet rays of sunlight."

"Aw, who cares for what the Doc says?" snorted some one in the crowd. "He's in cahoots with Dracula, anyhow!"

"I care," announced the calm voice of old Dr. Porter. "I know about that disease. If this gentleman has it, he is certainly wise to keep out of the sunlight. And, Dr. Crane, I wouldn't be surprised if you were right about Mary, too. Give me your re-volver, and I'll help guard the body, on my professional word of honor."

10. The Showdown

The younger doctor handed over his gun without an instant's hesitation, and started to work on the un-conscious form of Mary Morton, while Dr. Porter, Larousse, Higgins and Dan Callahan guarded the coffin on four sides.

"You're licked, Herman!" asserted Dan triumphantly.

"Not yet," muttered Fulton to himself, then aloud, "We are willing to listen to your explanations, Mr. Wilson, or Larousse, or whatever your name is. You have stated that some strange disease has made a night-prowler out of you. But where do you hole-up in the daytime? Answer me that."

"Very simple," replied the foreigner imperturbably. "I stay with Miss Harriet Wilson, the old lady whom you call 'Aunt Hattie,' and she really *is* my aunt, a much younger sister of my father."

The station agent now took a hand in the conversation.

"How do you explain all them little bats that hung around your coffin, the night we moved it for you?" he asked.

"Doubtless attracted by some of the embalming spices."

"And that *large bat?*"

"I didn't see any large bat?'

"*You* wouldn't," exclaimed the station agent triumphantly, "for he was you yourself. Haw! Haw! Haw!"

"Any further questions?" inquired Larousse, ignoring this sally.

"Yes," replied Herman Fulton, returning to the fray. "*Where* have you been hiding ever since Mary Morton died?"

"Not that it's any concern of yours, *but* I happen to have been in Philadelphia, *arranging* for a fitting headstone for my father's grave," explained the gentleman.

"That's right," asserted the station agent; "for, come to think of it, the way-bills for a headstone come in today. That is they come in yesterday, for I suppose today is tomorrow by now."

A few red streaks began to show in the eastern sky. Larousse at once became visibly agitated.

"Really, doctor," he said. "I hate to desert you at such a time. The dermatitis, you know. I must hurry away before it gets light. Here, take my revolver. You can keep it, and you can keep Higgins too, as long as you need them. I'd do anything for the sake of little Mary — except risk my damnable health."

"I know," sighed Dr. Crane, looking up from his work, and accepting the proffered firearm.

"And *we* know, too," sneered Herman Fulton. "Follow him to the Wilson lot, some of you men, and watch him ooze into the grave with the first beams of the rising sun."

"I think it would be safer, sir, for you to take your revolver with you," asserted Dr. Crane, handing back the pearl-handled thirty-two. "When daylight comes, I am sure that Dr. Porter and Dan and Higgins will be able to handle this bunch of fat-heads. Goodbye, and God bless you. I thank you for your help this night."

"Good-bye," replied Larousse. "Higgins will bring me word of the little lady. Goodbye, you swine. You *chameaux!*"

It was the supreme French insult. Wrapping his cloak about him, he strode majestically away.

"To the Wilson lot! Follow him!" shouted Herman Fulton.

But that was not the path which the tall stranger took. Instead he walked resolutely down toward the road.

"Follow him!" shrieked Herman, "Don't let him make his getaway! My God! Here we are trying to rid the world of a menace, and a nosy young doctor has to interfere and spoil it all. Come on. Never mind Mary. We must capture Dracula himself before he escapes us."

Whereupon he and the whole crowd, with the fickleness characteristic of mobs, rushed headlong after the retreating figure.

"The master needs me!" exclaimed Higgins, and followed in the wake of the mob.

"You go too, Dan," urged Ralph Crane. "Dr. Porter and I will be safe here, until those lynchers return."

So Dan Callahan hurried after Higgins.

As the crowd neared Larousse, those in the lead picked up stones and began to throw them. One stone grazed the cloaked figure, now clearly discernible in the gray morning light. Instantly Larousse wheeled and faced his tormentors.

"None of that!" he shouted. "I am a crack shot. I don't wish to fire at you, but I shall certainly do it if you make it necessary."

"Arrr," howled the mob, and let fly a shower of stones, several of which hit him squarely.

But he stood his ground. Instead of giving way, he raised his pearl-handled revolver and pointed it steadily at them.

"Aw, what do we care for toy pistols," shouted one of the men, raising a stone aloft and preparing to hurl it.

"Crack!" went the tall stranger's little weapon. The stone clattered to the ground, as the man who had been about to hurl it clapped his left hand to his right wrist, from which the blood was spurting

"I warned you that I was a crack shot," repeated Larousse levelly, "and I meant it. Raise another stone against me, and I swear I shall shoot to kill."

Contemptuously he turned his back on them, and resumed his march to the road.

From a safe position in the rear of the mob, Herman Fulton urged, "Don't let him get away! Throw a lot of rocks quick, before he can turn!"

Something hard and small and cylindrical poked Herman suddenly in the ribs from behind, and Dan Callahan's voice spoke in his ear, "Quick! Tell them *not* to throw any rocks."

Herman did so, promptly, in a trembling voice. Higgins dashed through the crowd to his master's side.

Said Herman, "You'll be sorry for this, Callahan. No one ever bucks me in this town, and gets away with it. The mortgage on your garage is overdue."

"Forget it!" exclaimed Dan jovially. "When this gang finds out that you've made monkeys out of them tonight, I guess you won't be foreclosing any mortgages around here for quite a while. You may *control* a majority of the stock in the bank, but you don't *own* it. And Dr. Porter, your largest stockholder, is on *our* side now. Put that in your pipe and smoke it!"

"Oh, Dan," wailed Herman, "can't you see what you're doing? We're trying to rid the world of a menace, and you and that half-witted doctor — "

The revolver bored dangerously into his ribs.

"One more wise-crack out of you, you skunk," announced Dan, "and I'll be making the world safe for mortgages."

Meanwhile Larousse and his chauffeur Higgins had reached their parked car, closely followed by the threatening mob. Then, while Higgins stood them off, his employer climbed into the driver's seat, and started down the road, Higgins jumping to the running-board as he departed.

Herman Fulton was about to wail again, but a sharp jab in the ribs from Callahan's revolver kept him quiet.

Several others of the mob, however, hastened to their own cars, and soon were off down the road in pursuit of Larousse. It was now daylight, with the rim of the sun just showing above the tops of the eastern hills.

"Back to *Mary's* grave!" shouted someone, whereupon the rest of the mob wheeled, and started back across the cemetery.

"None of that!" shouted Callahan, standing in their path with levelled revolver.

The spirit of the mob collapsed. They gazed sheepishly at each other. It was daylight now, broad daylight. The anonymity of the night was at an end. The darkness had covered them like the mask and robe of the Ku Klux, but now they stood exposed and undisguised.

I t isn't exactly a dignified performance for a lot of leading businessmen, and church elders, and bank directors, and coal miners, and what-not, of a conservative Republican community, however benighted and backwoodsy it may be, to dig up a body in a churchyard in the dead of night. And being caught still at it in broad daylight is even worse. They were ashamed of themselves and of each other.

In the midst of their confusion, young Dr. Crane and old Dr. Porter, standing by the coffin, beckoned to them, and then advanced to meet them, Crane holding his revolver again.

"She is alive," announced the older man, "but she is very weak. At present she is asleep. We must carry her back to town at once, and have a blood-transfusion."

"She called your name, Herman," added Dr. Crane, grimly. "It was the first thing she said when she came to. "

Herman appeared visibly shaken at this announcement. Also his faith in the weird ideas gleaned from his reading was somewhat shaken as well

"I'll call a truce," said he. "It's now daylight. The vampire, if she is a vampire, is at our mercy until sunset. We can lose nothing by giving in temporarily to the two doctors."

"If my daughter is really alive," began Pop Morton emphatically. And then suddenly he remembered the mortgage on his stock of goods, and became quiet again.

Ralph Crane replied to Herman Fulton's offer. Said he, toying with his gun, "We accept your truce, but with reservations. We are armed and we intend to stay armed until we see this thing through. We've been handed treachery before by you folks, and So we are taking no chances. Mary is very weak; she must be moved immediately, but quietly. The coffin and the hearse — gruesome as it sounds — will be the best way to move her. So I want six — ah — *un*-pallbearers, one might say," he laughed grimly, "to assist. Fulton and Morton — the job will keep you two out of mischief — Crocker, Warren, Crosby and Banks." He named the last four at random. "The rest of you lunatics keep out of the way, and heaven help you if you interfere. Come on, you six, and the undertaker."

So saying, he led the way back to the grave. It was a nerve-racking experience for the six "un-pallbearers." They had served at funerals before, all of them, and had thought nothing of it; had even jested, sedately, on such occasions, across the body. But never before had they spent an entire night in exhuming a corpse, only to carry it back to town with them — either alive or "un-dead" — whichever it was — in the morning.

It seemed for all the world, as though their actions were actually being run backward, like a trick motion-picture film. But it was their dread of ridicule that worried them, rather than any dread of the super-natural. Broad daylight had arrived, and their antics of the preceding night now seemed preposterous to them. They felt uneasy and conspicuous.

These men, who had been game to dig up a poor girl's body, drive a stake through her heart, cut off her head, and stuff her mouth full of garlic, now balked at the mere task of carrying her back to life again! But they had no choice in the matter. Dr. Crane and his supporters held the revolvers.

Without mishap, they got the coffin onto the hearse, which happened to be there merely because it was the undertaker's only means of personal conveyance. The rest of the mob rapidly and sheepishly disintegrated, all except Herman Fulton and one or two others, whose mortgages were the most hopelessly overdue.

Just as they were about to start for town, an automobile drew up, driven by one of the men who had pursued "Dracula."

He reported to Herman, 'We followed the old boy to Aunt Hattie's cottage. By the time we got there, he was inside, and his chauffeur was on guard at the door with a gat in his hand. Our crowd just plain got cold feet, and went home. So I came back to report to you."

"But are you sure that Dracula is still inside Aunt Hattie's house?" asked Herman Fulton eagerly.

11. A New Victim

N-no," admitted the other, "but he must be, for his chauffeur and his car are there."

"Then he probably has a coffin at the cottage, as well as in the grave in the Wilson lot," asserted Herman positively; "for vampires always have to sleep in coffins in the daytime. Well, he's safe for the present. Let's get Mary's body back to town, and see how *that* turns out. Then we can tend to the old boy later in the day."

His mind still failed to grasp the fact that his little lynching-bee was over, at least for the present.

So the hearse started toward town. Dan Callahan, with drawn revolver, sat on the seat beside the undertaker. The two doctors rode in the rear with the coffin, Crane still holding his revolver. Herman Fulton followed in his own car at a safe distance. Also the six un-pallbearers.

The return to town was uneventful, and in a few minutes the hearse drew up at the Morton residence. The un-pallbearers came forward, the coffin was carried in, and the pale sleeping form of Mary Morton was lifted out and transferred to her bed. She was pale now because at the grave the two doctors had washed off her rouge, so as to be able to observe her true color.

Then Dr. Porter got the village nurse on the phone, she arrived with a lot of paraphernalia, and preparations were made for an immediate blood-transfusion.

Dr. Crane, Pop Morton and Dan Callahan were each tested as a possible donor, but their bloods all gave the wrong reaction.

"Herman," announced old Dr. Porter, "you are elected for the next test."

Herman Fulton turned pale.

"But I read in that book," he stammered, "that an interchange of blood with a vampire will tie a person to the vampire forever. Oh, Dr. Porter, please don't! If I give Mary some of my blood, and then she dies, it will mean that I must look forward all my life to being a vampire myself when I finally die!"

"Rubbish!" exclaimed Dr. Porter, impatiently.

"Can't you use a salt and glucose solution?" Herman persisted. "I've read somewhere that it's just as good as real blood for transfusions."

"You read altogether too much!" snorted the old doctor. "Saline solution is no good in anemia. What she needs is red blood corpuscles, and the needs them in a hurry."

"The trouble with Herman is that he's a highbrow," added Dan. "He's educated beyond his intelligence.'

"Herman," said Pop Morton levelly, "you are engaged to my daughter. Didn't you say something, up at the grave, about your having the first right to save her? Well, now's your chance, and if you don't take it, the engagement is off, mortgage or no mortgage!"

During Pop's remarks, Fulton had been getting all ready to mention the mortgage, but now Pop had got in ahead of him. Fulton squirmed visibly.

'Well," said he finally, "go ahead and make the test. Maybe *my* blood won't be the right kind either."

But, alas for Herman, his blood turned out to be in exactly the same class as Mary's. He paled again.

"It's murder!" he screamed. "It's worse than murder!"

But his captors were inexorable. While Dr. Crane held a pistol to his head Dan Callahan, grinning broadly, forced him into a chair and strapped him down.

"There's one comfort, Herman," said Dan: "if you turn into a vampire when you die it will give me great pleasure to drive a stake through your filthy heart, and cut off your head, and stuff your mouth full of vegetables. Then think how happy you'll be! I believe you yourself got off some such pious sentiment about little Mary. We want you to be happy, Herman dear, the same as you wanted Mary to be."

"This is no joking matter," Fulton blubbered.

"Now, now, Herman," soothed the Irishman, "shall we gag you, or will you keep quiet?"

"Don't gag him," objected Dr. Crane. "It might startle Mary. In fact we'd better even untie him. You stand out of Mary's sight, Dan, and cover him with your gun. If he let's out a yip, you shoot. I mean it, Herman, for I'm just about fed up with you."

Then he and Dan carried their trussed-up victim, white but silent, into the sick-room, where they untied him. In another moment, two arms were antisepticized, and soon the blood was flowing from Herman Fulton's forearm through a little rubber tube into Mary Morton's.

Herman watched the performance like one hypnotized. He saw Mary's color return, as she fed upon his lifeblood. All his worst fears had come to pass. This vampire, whom he had set out to slay, the evening before, was now feasting upon him; but, instead of perching on his body with two sharp white teeth piercing his throat, she was lying luxuriously in bed, while two up-to-date doctors were doing all the work of the transfusion. What a strange modernizing of medieval superstition! Herman even felt himself under the influence of that lethargic stupor which — from his reading — he well knew that vampires are able to produce in their victims.

Meanwhile several of Herman's staunchest henchmen gathered outside.

Old Dr. Porter viewed them from the window of the sick-room; then turning back, he announced, "We're not out of the woods yet. In addition to all the trouble we're having with our patient, the mob may get up its courage again before we are through."

"Sit," admonished the younger doctor. "Mary is coming out of her trance again."

As Herman grew weaker and weaker, the flush of health gradually spread over Mary's features. She stirred in the bed, and opened her eyes.

"Herman," she breathed, "where am I? I had a most awful dream. I dreamed that I was dead and buried, and that you came and dug me up. What's this on my arm? And all these doctors and a nurse! What's it all about, father?"

But Dr. Porter, admonishing the others to silence, said, "You've been very sick, Mary. But we've given you a blood-transfusion, and you're all right now."

"Herman, dear," said the girl, as she turned a beatific smile toward her fiancé, "you gave your blood to save my life. I remember calling for you in my dream. I left the grave, and came and stood by your bed, and begged you to help me. You seemed frightened or horrified then; I could not tell which. But you *did* come. You love me very much, dear, don't you?"

Fulton hung his head in shame, and said nothing.

Dr. Porter announced bruskly, "The patient must have absolute rest for a while. Everyone, except the nurse, must go now — even the beloved Herman."

Fulton glowered at him, but obediently left the room with the others, Mary's trusting glance lingering on him as he went.

As soon as he was outside, the old doctor whispered to him, "You'd better get to bed, Herman. You're a very weak man, just now."

"You can go right to bed here in our spare room," offered Mary's father, hospitably.

To which Dr. Crane added, "Fine! Then we can keep our eyes on him."

Herman, however, needed no surveillance. He was weak and shaken. He was through — at least for the present. So far as he was concerned, old Dracula could go to the devil! Herman himself wanted to go to bed. So he did.

But Herman Fulton was not permanently defeated. He had merely suffered a temporary setback. He was merely weak from loss of blood. But he was still president of the Yankton Bank. He still held most of the overdue mortgages in town. He was still engaged to Mary Morton. And she still adoringly regarded him as her rescuer.

12. The Denouement

By evening, Herman Fulton had completely recovered his poise. What ever might be his future plans for combatting the Dracula menace, he realized that for the present it would pay him to dissemble, and to try and make friends with the enemy.

So he warmly, and with apparent sincerity, urged Ralph Crane to return to his Yankton practice. But the young doctor declined. He could not bear to stay and see his Mary, whose life he himself had saved, happily give herself in marriage to the man who had tried to kill her.

"Herman," said he, after refusing the other's offer, "for once you can put your fiendish mortgage-system to a good use. Let it be known by every participant of last night's attempted outrage, that if the least hint of it ever reaches Miss Morton's ears, you will run the person responsible out of town."

Just then Peter Larousse was announced. He had come to inquire as to the health of the patient. The two doctors reported that Mary was already greatly improved under the new line of treatment, based on Dr. Crane's diagnosis.

Then Herman asked a bit apprehensively what Larousse's plans were.

"You will be relieved to know," the old man replied with dignity, "that I am at once shaking the dust of this town off my feet forever. How my father could ever have felt any affection for Yankton, is beyond my comprehension. But I have carried out his wishes, and have buried him here.

> Here he lies where he longed to be,
> Horne is the sailor, home from the see,
> And the hunter home from the hill.

"But, as for me," Larousse continued, "I am moving tonight back to civilization. Dr. Crane, I am going to accept your offer, made when I first came here, to treat my dermatitis. I shall put up at your hospital in New York. You have won my respect. And there are two other people in this town who are deserving of respect, namely, Miss Morton and the taxi-man. I still mistrust you, Mr. Fulton, for a dangerous idiot. So I shall instruct my solicitors to pay off the Callahan and Morton mortgages."

"God bless you, sir; you're a brick!" exclaimed the young Irishman.

"Why — why — why," stammered Pop Morton. "Why, it'll put me on my feet for the first time in years! You can't realize what it means to me, Mr. Dracula — uh, I mean, Mr. Larousse."

Herman Fulton looked daggers at this man who dared to free two victims from his (Herman's) clutches.

Larousse continued, "Dr. Porter, I hope that you will use your bank-stock to curb Mr. Fulton's impetuosity. And of course, I assume that Miss Morton has broken, or will break, her engagement?"

"Unfortunately no," replied Dr. Crane bitterly. "She credits her fiancé with last night's rescue."

Herman hung his head.

"And you don't propose to disillusion her?" asked Larousse in surprise.

"Why should I?" countered Crane. "She loves Herman, so it would be best for her never to know the truth."

"Doctor Crane," remonstrated Dan Callahan, "if you'll excuse my impertinence, I think you're all wet. You've got Herman by the tail now, so why not give it a twist? If I were you, sir, I'd tell Miss Morton all the facts. Begging your pardon, sir, but she loves you, and you love her, and she's only marrying that skunk out of loyalty and mistaken gratitude."

"What?" exclaimed Herman Fulton and Pop Morton in unison.

The young doctor colored.

"No, no, Dan," he remonstrated, "you are mistaken. Miss Morton and I are merely warm friends; that is all. If there is even any suspicion of anything else, it is just as well that I am leaving town for good."

"Yes, I agree with you," interposed Herman, a bit too enthusiastically.

Dr. Crane glowered at him.

Dan Callahan snorted with disgust.

"I'm beginning to think," he averred, "that there's only two people in this town that ain't crazy; me and Mr. Larousse. Thank you again, Mr. Larousse, for fixing up my mortgage so that I can stay right in Yankton and make Herman Fulton watch his step. I'll pay you back some day, sir. And as for you, Doctor Crane, I hope you'll come to your senses before it's too late. So long, everybody."

And he stalked out.

Pop Morton, Monsieur Larousse, Herman Fulton, and the two doctors tried to keep up conversation for a while, but at last it lagged. Every one except "old Dracula" felt tense and embarrassed.

At last Dr. Crane remarked, "Well, it's almost time for the night train east. If Doctor Porter doesn't mind, I think I'll go upstairs and say good-bye to Mary."

The older doctor nodded, and young Crane passed from the room.

He found the nurse standing by Miss Morton's door with an amused smile on her face. She opened the door for him, but discreetly remained outside.

Mary was sitting up in bed, pale but smiling. Crane advanced toward her eagerly.

And then he noticed that they were not alone.

"What on earth are *you* doing here, Callahan?" he demanded, coming to a halt.

But it was Mary who answered.

"He's been telling me the truth, Ralph," said she. "Oh, Ralph, you poor dear silly noble-minded old darling! Why did you want me to marry a superstitious moron, who tried to kill me, instead of yourself, who saved my life? Ralph, dear, I've loved you ever since you came to town, but I haven't realized it until right now."

And she held out her arms to the astonished young doctor.

"Take it or leave it, Doc," said Dan Callahan, with a grin, as he walked out
of the room.

And Dr. Crane took it.

Ralph Milne Farley was a pseudonym for Roger Sherman Hoar (April 8, 1887 - October 10, 1963), a US constitutional lawyer, politician, teacher, and author. Under his given name he wrote several books on taxes, patents, insurance, and law. Under the Farley name he published hundreds of short stories, novellas, poems, and essays in pulp magazines. He was best known for his Radio Man series.

Curtis Charles (C.C.) Senf (July 30, 1873 - April 24, 1949) was born in Prussia and emigrated to the U.S as a child with his family. After attending the Chicago Art Institute he embarked on a career as a graphic illustrator producing work for the Chicago advertising industry. Between 1927 and 1932 Senf drew hundreds of black and white interior illustrations and painted forty-five covers for Weird Tales magazine.

www.ingramcontent.com/pod-product-compliance
Lightning Source LLC
Chambersburg PA
CBHW060509300726
48975CB00008B/2706